C00 033 019X

D1632457

# THE GREEN MAN

written by      illustrated by
### Bel Mooney & Helen Cann

BAREFOOT BOOKS

BATH

# THE GREEN MAN

Once there was a boy called Luke, who lived in a flat in the city. One winter morning Luke got up, looked out of his window, and saw the world all grey. The road, the pavement, the buildings, the sky – all grey. It hadn't changed. It was always like that. But today Luke noticed it for the first time. And all the window boxes on the block of flats were empty.

At breakfast Luke's Dad hid behind sheets of grey newspaper. His Mum poured brown cereal into a white bowl, and the milk turned a greyish brown.
'Mum,' asked Luke, 'Why do we have plastic flowers on the table?'
'Because they never die,' Mum replied. 'And they are easy to look after.'
Luke put out a finger, touched a hard grey-green leaf, and thought.

Later that day, Luke and his mother went shopping. They parked the car in the multi-storey car park, then set off to the supermarket. Buses, vans, cars and lorries whizzed past them as they waited to cross the road. There was a scrubby old tree near the traffic light, growing out of a hole in the pavement. Luke looked twice at the tree and couldn't believe what he saw.

A man's face was watching him, all rough and gnarled like the bark itself – but green. Leaves and tendrils formed his hair, and more leaves sprouted from his ears and his mouth. He looked very fierce and Luke felt afraid. 'Look, Mum!' he whispered. But as he spoke, the lights changed, and Mum led him across the road. When he turned round to have another look all he could see was a patch of dirty lichen on the tree trunk.

They went into the supermarket. Mum clutched her shopping list and frowned. Luke pushed the trolley, and Mum put in tins and bottles. They came to the vegetables, and she picked up a tray of tomatoes. Then a box of mushrooms. Then a plastic bag of lettuce. Luke was looking at a wrapped cabbage – when suddenly it blinked. He stared in amazement at a face in the leaves, all curling and green. 'Look, Mum!' he whispered. 'There's a man's face in that cabbage. A green face!'

'Don't be silly, Luke,' said Mum.

Luke felt scared. 'But, Mum, I can see him,' he insisted.

'See who, Luke?' asked Mum.

'The Green Man – look there on the cabbage!' Luke replied.

Mum picked up the cabbage, and gave Luke a very funny look. 'It's just a cabbage Luke, and to prove it we'll eat it tonight with lamb chops and gravy.' She threw the cabbage into the trolley. When Luke looked again the face had disappeared.

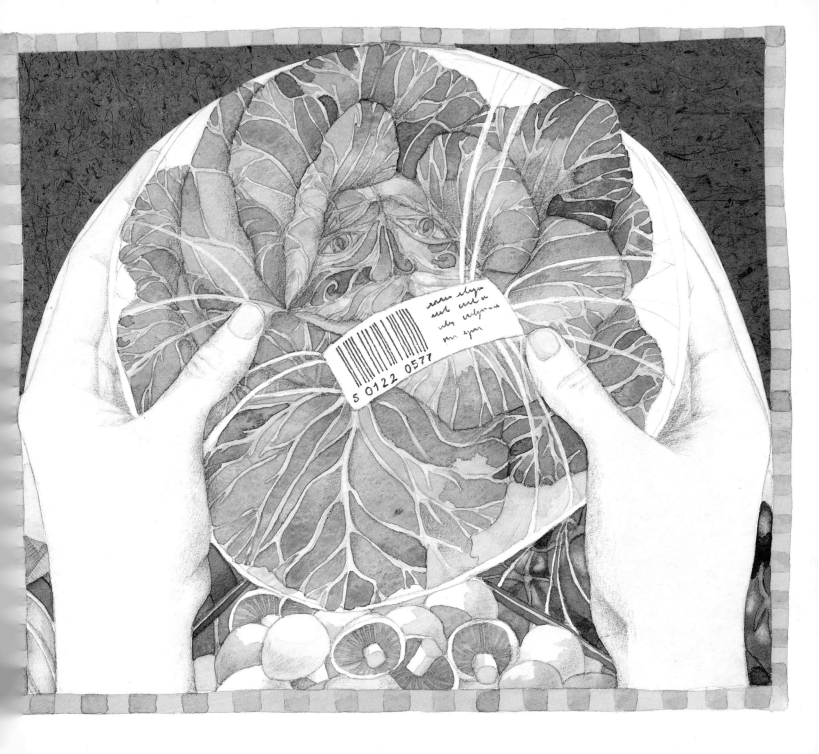

On the way home Luke was very quiet. He was almost afraid to look around in case he saw that green face again. But why should he feel so frightened? The face had been friendly – *quite*. It had seemed as if it wanted to talk to him. Suddenly he felt he had to see the man again. As they sped by he looked at the trees at the side of the road, the hedges, the railings

of the park. He didn't spot the Green Man, but for the first time he noticed other things. He
saw the new flyover in the distance, with cars crawling over it like insects on an elephant's
back. He saw tall blocks of flats, with nowhere for the children to play. He saw the huge
new shopping centre where once there had been green fields. It was all so UGLY.

'Mum – why are they always building shops and carparks and roads?' he asked.

'Oh, who knows?' sighed Mum.

'Somebody must know!' cried Luke.

'Well, it's progress, isn't it?' said his mother, tooting her horn at the car in front.

Luke frowned. *That* didn't seem a good answer at all.

Behind the block of flats where they lived were rows of gardens, but nobody bothered to grow plants there anymore. As Luke was helping Mum carry the shopping up the path, he stopped suddenly.

There was a straggly bush just by the path, and in it – was the Green Man again! This time the green face was smiling openly, as if to say, 'I surprised you this time!'

Luke went up to him.

'Do those leaves choke you?' asked Luke.

'No, they just make it hard to talk!' mumbled the green face.

'Luke!' Mum shouted, 'Hurry up, and stop talking to yourself.'

'I'm not talking to myself – come and look! It's that face again. Look there!'

'That's just an old bush,' said Mum impatiently.

Inside, Mum asked Luke to set the table for tea. 'I need that big plate with all the roses on it,' she said, 'Go and fetch it.' Luke went to the sideboard – and in the swirling brown grain of the wood, he saw the leafy face again. 'Why are you following me?' Luke asked quietly. In his mind he thought he heard a deep voice whisper, 'Wait.'

That night Luke dreamed of the Green Man. He was searching for him everywhere, but the leafy face didn't appear. In despair, he sat down by the side of the road and cried. But as he looked down a little crack appeared in the concrete. Then another. Then another.

It was like an earthquake – the ground splitting before his eyes. A leafy tendril curled out of the crack – followed by more and more greenery. He saw a green eye, a green cheek, branches pouring from the mouth. Then the green man pulled his whole body out of the hole in the road, and held out a hand.
'Come with me,' said the Green Man. Luke knew he had never been so happy in his whole life. Then he woke up.

That morning the sun was shining. Luke went out to play, but there were no other children in the street. Aimlessly he wandered about, and suddenly noticed an opening in the concrete wall at the back of the estate. Leading from it was a narrow path with a fence each side. Luke had never seen it before. He wandered up the path and found himself standing by an old shed, its green paint peeling. Today it didn't surprise him to see that face again.

'Hello, Green Man!' he said happily, 'But why is it nobody else can see you, only me?'

'Oh, but I can see him too!' exclaimed a voice.

Luke jumped. A round, rosy face was looking at him through the dirty shed window. It disappeared, and then the whole person appeared at the door. It was the strangest old woman Luke had ever seen. She wore an old yellow hat, with a red flower stuck in it, a bright blue jacket over a pink jumper, and a skirt striped with all the colours of the rainbow. There were big brown boots on her feet, and she was holding a spade.

'Hello, my name's Lily,' she said.

'I'm Luke,' he replied. Her hand was as rough as bark.

Luke saw that they were standing in a sort of garden. 'Do you like my allotment?' asked Lily. 'The Green Man helps me grow things here. I've got potatoes and carrots and turnips coming up, and there'll be peas and beans and courgettes … and masses of brilliant flowers! Look!' She pointed to the ground, and Luke saw green shoots all around them. Luke felt something spring up inside him, as if a green shoot was growing there too.

'But who *is* the Green Man?' he asked.

Lily sat down on an old bench by the shed door, and Luke sat with her. 'He's the oldest spirit in the world,' she explained. 'He was here even before the mountains and seas were made, I reckon. He's trees and flowers and corn and weeds and jungles and, and … oh, he's all growing things in one, and everything grows because of him.'

'But why does he sometimes look fierce?' asked Luke.

'Because people try to ignore him of course!' said Lily, 'Look around you.' She pointed at the tall grey buildings and roads in the distance and sighed. 'But the amazing thing is – the Green Man will never go away. Not ever. He's been here for too long!'

'Why do I keep seeing him all over the place? Why me?' asked Luke.

'I saw him when I was your age,' Lily told him, 'But that was years ago, and lots of people knew about him then. But as I got older, things changed. People cut down the trees, built houses, roads and shops, and nobody thought it mattered. So I suppose the Green Man went underground. It seems he only appears to people he thinks will help him. And, Luke, he's chosen *you*.'

'But what am I supposed to do?' asked Luke.

Lily stood up, and held out a hand. With the other hand she opened the shed door, and pointed. 'There you are!' she said triumphantly, 'It's all inside.'

Luke gasped. The shed looked much bigger inside than it did from outside, and it was completely lined with shelves. There were packets of seed, and sacks of bulbs, and trays with green shoots sprouting through the soil. There were piles of empty earthenware plant pots,

and rows of other pots with plants in them. There were trowels and forks and green string in rolls and things like scissors, and watering cans, and baskets, and bags of compost. Luke breathed in deeply. The air smelt of warmth and soil and growth. 'We've got work to do,' Lily declared.

Much later, Lily and Luke walked slowly back to the flats. Lily pushed a wheelbarrow full of trays, seeds, bulbs and gardening equipment. She looked at the dreary empty gardens and shook her head. 'We'll soon change all that,' said Luke with a grin. His hands were dirty, and his back ached a bit – but he felt very happy. He raced upstairs to tell Mum and Dad about his adventure, then rushed out again. Lily had already started to dig. People were looking out of their windows in amazement at the sight.

At last Mum and Dad couldn't resist coming down, and started to help. Soon there were lots of little rows, with seed packets on sticks at the ends. 'The seeds will soon grow,' explained Lily, 'And when everybody sees how pretty your plot looks, they'll dig their own patches. You wait and see. Soon it will all be green.'

'It will be nice to have real flowers in the house,' admitted Luke's Mum.

'When I was a kid we had fresh fruit and vegetables, not those supermarket varieties, and I remember how good they tasted,' said Luke's Dad excitedly.

They all went upstairs for tea, and when Luke looked down at the rose plate he caught Lily's eye and winked. 'Don't forget to do your last bit of planting before bed,' she whispered.

In his pyjamas, Luke opened his bedroom window, put some earth in the empty window box, and sprinkled flower seeds on top. 'Will you grow?' he whispered. As he drifted off to sleep he could smell soil and damp leaves and flowers.

The morning sun filled Luke's room with greeny-gold light. As he sat up in bed, he gasped with joy. His window box was full of tall flowers, red, yellow, blue and white, which nodded and waved their leaves in the breeze. Thick tendrils of ivy curled all round his window, fringing it with leaves – just like the hair of the Green Man.

'I don't believe it!' he cried with delight. 'Did I really do that?'

Then he heard the Green Man's voice, 'You see it's true, Luke! Trust me – you can make things different!'

# AUTHOR'S NOTE

Nobody knows where the Green Man comes from. I first saw him carved on the end of a bench in a country church – a rough face with vines curling out of his mouth, and leaves in his hair. Then I saw him again and again, in stone, in wood, sometimes looking sad, sometimes quite scary. On holiday in France, I came across him in a few churches, and once in Italy, carved by a door. In a church in Wiltshire he has birds nesting in his leafy hair. With the leaves spurting out of his mouth it almost looks as if he is giving birth to the natural world.

Wanting to find out more about him, I discovered that he stands for something so old nobody quite understands it. All we know is that when churches were built, country people believed in the Green Man – a belief older than the Christian faith. So the priests let them carve him all over the place – just to be sure, you see. Because he stands for harvest, crops, trees, plant life, growth – Nature itself, going on and on. He is a spirit, but he is real too – as soft as rain on crops, as hard as winter. He is friendly, but fierce too – if you don't treat him well. The Green Man is as real today as he was for our ancestors hundreds of years ago, even though most people have forgotten what their great great grandparents knew. You may live in the city, but you touch the Green Man when you grow plants on your windowsill, or take autumn leaves to school. People from town and country alike speak for him when they shout out that hedges, wild flowers and trees, and all the birds and little creatures who live in them, matter. Imagine a world covered up with concrete, with no room for growth or wildness!

If you worry about the destruction of our lovely earth like I do, you will know that the Green Man stands for the sacredness of nature. He is there in the trees, the bushes and the plants of our native countryside, and in the rainforests, the mountains and the marshes. If you listen closely you may hear him begging, 'Look around you, love what you see – and please take care of it, before you lose it forever.'

*Bel Mooney, 1997*

Barefoot Books, PO Box 95, Kingswood, Bristol BS15 5BH. Text copyright © 1997 by Bel Mooney. Illustrations copyright © 1997 by Helen Cann. First published in Great Britain in 1997 by Barefoot Books Ltd. All rights reserved. No part of this book may be reproduced in any form or by any means, electronic or mechanical, including photocopying, recording, or by an information storage and retrieval system, without permission in writing from the publisher. British Library Cataloguing-in-Publication Data. A catalogue record for this book is available from the British Library. ISBN 1 898000 98 0